A Little Princess

My First Classics

The Secret Garden

by Frances Hodgson Burnett,

adapted by Laura F. Marsh

My First Classics

A Little Princess

BY FRANCES HODGSON BURNETT

ADAPTED BY LAURA F. MARSH

HarperFestival®

A Division of HarperCollinsPublishers

My First Classics: A Little Princess
Copyright © 2005 by HarperCollins Publishers, Inc.
Printed in the United States of America.
For information address HarperCollins Children's Books, a division of HarperCollins
Publishers, 1350 Avenue of the Americas, New York, NY 10019.
www.harperchildrens.com
Library of Congress catalog card number: 2004111657
Typography by Tom Starace
1 2 3 4 5 6 7 8 9 10
❖
First HarperFestival edition, 2005

Contents

~ 1 ~
Sara

On a dark winter's day a little girl sat in a carriage with her father as they drove through the streets of London. Her father had his arm around her.

Seven-year-old Sara Crewe looked with big eyes at the people passing by. She had just sailed from her home in Bombay, India, with her father, Captain Crewe. Sara noticed that London looked different than India. Bombay was hot and bright with sun. London during the day looked as dark as night. As they passed shop windows, she saw the lamps blaze as if it were evening, and the fog hung thick and heavy in the streets.

"Papa, is this the place?" Sara whispered.

"Yes, little Sara, it is," he said sadly.

Sara had known for a long time she would make this trip. It was so hot in India that many people believed it was not a good place for children. Lots of children Sara knew went to school in England. She had known someday she would, too. Sara's only worry was that her father could not stay with her.

Sara's mother died when Sara was a baby, and so Sara never knew her. Sara loved her father dearly. He was the only family she had. He, too, loved Sara with all his heart and liked to call her his "Little Missus."

Sara had heard people say her father was rich. Though she did not really know what this meant, she knew there was nothing she could not have.

"You will go live in a nice house with a lot of other girls to play with," her father had said about school. "Before long, it will be time to come home to Papa."

Sara liked to think of returning to her father and taking care of him. That is what she wanted most in the world. And if she needed to go away to England to do this, she would.

"Well, Papa, if we are here, I guess I'm ready."

He laughed as he kissed her. He was not sure he was ready to let Sara go. His sweet little girl had been a wonderful companion to him, and he knew he would be lonely when he returned to India. So he held her tightly in his arms.

When the carriage stopped, Sara and her father were in front of a big, dull, brick house, just like all of the others in its row. On the front door was a sign:

MISS MINCHIN

SELECT SCHOOL FOR YOUNG LADIES

Captain Crewe lifted Sara out of the cab and they climbed the steps. Sara often thought afterward how the school was like Miss Minchin herself: neat and fancy, but also as stiff, unpleasant, and uncomfortable as the furniture. As she sat down in a hard wooden chair, Sara looked around.

"I don't like it, Papa," she said, "but I know soldiers don't like going into battle, either." Captain Crewe was a captain in the British army. She must be brave like him now.

Her father swept little Sara into his arms and kissed her. She saw tears come to his eyes.

Just then Miss Minchin walked into the room. She had a cold, fishy smile. Miss Minchin had heard many things about Captain Crewe. Most of all, she had heard he was rich.

"It will be an honor to care for such a beautiful and clever child," she said. "Sara will be a treasure to this school."

Sara did not know she was pretty. She had an odd charm about her, with her dark black hair and big green eyes. Later Sara discovered Miss Minchin said this about every child who walked through her doors.

As her father and Miss Minchin talked, Sara thought of what her life would be like now. She was to have a pretty bedroom and a sitting room, a pony and a carriage, and a maid of her own. This was more than the other girls at school had.

"It will be difficult to keep Sara from learning too much too quickly," Captain Crewe said to Miss Minchin. "She always has her nose in a book. Make sure she plays, as well. She can ride her pony or buy a new doll."

"But if I bought many more dolls," said Sara, "I would have too many to like. Dolls should be close friends. Emily is going to be my closest friend."

"Who is Emily?" asked Miss Minchin.

"She is a doll I haven't gotten yet," said Sara. "She will be my friend when Papa is gone."

Miss Minchin's large, stiff smile crept across her face. "What a darling little girl!"

"Yes," said Captain Crewe, "she is. Please take good care of her, Miss Minchin." Captain Crewe said that Sara was to have everything she asked for and Miss Minchin was to send him the bills.

Sara stayed with her father at his hotel for several days before he returned to India. The two went shopping and Captain Crewe bought Sara velvet dresses with expensive furs, hats with great big feathers, and boxes of gloves and lace stockings. The women in the stores thought the little girl must be a princess.

And after looking in many shops, at last they found Emily.

"Oh, Papa!" cried Sara, grabbing her father's arm. "There is Emily! I knew her the minute I saw her."

She was big, but not too large to carry. She had curly brown hair and deep blue eyes. Clothes were made for Emily, just as fancy as Sara's. Captain Crewe was glad Sara had Emily as a friend to keep her company while he was gone.

On the last day Sara and her father were together, they sat in her sitting room at the school. When it was time for Captain Crewe to leave, Sara told her father, "You are inside my heart." He hugged his "Little Missus" for a long time. Then Captain Crewe's carriage drove away as Sara looked after it.

When Miss Minchin sent up her sister, Miss Amelia, to check on Sara, Amelia found that Sara had locked the door. "I'd like to be by myself now, please," Sara said through the door.

"I've never known such a child," Amelia told Miss Minchin.

"I expected her to kick and scream the way many do," said Miss Minchin. "Especially since she's always gotten her way."

"And her clothes—" began Amelia.

"They are ridiculously fancy," interrupted Miss Minchin, "but they will look wonderful at the head of the line when we go to church on Sunday."

~ 2 ~

A French Lesson

When Sara walked into the schoolroom the next morning, all of the girls stared at her. By this time everyone had heard about Sara—how she had come from a faraway country and how her father was quite rich.

"She has silk stockings!" whispered a girl named Jessie.

Sara sat quietly in her seat near Miss Minchin's desk. She was not embarrassed by the girls' stares. Sara was interested in the other girls, too, and looked quietly back at them.

Miss Minchin rapped on her desk. "Young ladies, I wish to introduce you to your new friend, Miss Sara Crewe." All of the children stood up and bowed to Sara.

"Sara," said Miss Minchin, "since your papa hired a French maid for you, it seems he wishes you to learn French."

"I think he hired her because he thought I would like her, Miss Minchin," Sara said in a kind voice.

Miss Minchin forced a tight smile, "You have

been a spoiled girl. Things are not always done because you like them."

Sara wanted to explain to Miss Minchin, but she also wanted to be polite. The truth was that Sara could not remember a time when she did not speak French. Her mother was French, and Captain Crewe had always spoken the language with her.

"I have never really learned French, but—" said Sara.

"That is enough," Miss Minchin interrupted sharply.

Sara's cheeks felt warm. She opened the book Miss Minchin had given her and tried not to smile at the simple French words she was supposed to be learning.

When the French teacher arrived, Miss Minchin said to Monsieur Dufarge, "Sara's papa is anxious for her to learn the language, but I am afraid she does not wish to."

Little Sara stood up and spoke in fluent French to explain to Monsieur Dufarge that her mother and father had spoken French. She would be glad to learn anything he would teach her, but she already knew the words in the book she had been given.

Miss Minchin was shocked. She stared at Sara over her glasses. Monsieur Dufarge smiled with pleasure. To hear this pretty childish voice speaking his language made him feel as if he was home. He turned to Miss Minchin, "There is not much I can teach her. She has not learned French. She is French."

"You should have told me!" Miss Minchin said to Sara.

But Miss Minchin knew it was her fault that Sara had not been allowed to explain. From that moment on, Miss Minchin held a grudge against Sara for making her look foolish.

Ermengarde

During her first morning in school, Sara noticed a girl her age with blue eyes. She was biting her hair ribbon and staring at Sara with wonder. Since she had trouble with French, the girl was surprised to hear Sara speak the language so easily.

Miss Minchin was in a bad temper and spotted the girl.

"Miss St. John!" Miss Minchin said loudly. "What are you doing? Take your ribbon out of your mouth! Sit up at once!"

Miss St. John jumped in alarm. When Jessie and another girl, Lavinia, started whispering, she turned red and tears came to her eyes. Sara felt sorry for her and wanted to be her friend.

Throughout the morning, Sara saw that school was not easy for Miss St. John. Lavinia and Jessie giggled about her for being slow to learn. After classes were over and the girls were talking in groups, Sara went over to Miss St. John.

"What is your name?" she asked.

9

"My name is Ermengarde St. John," she answered.

"Mine is Sara Crewe," said Sara. "I like your name. It sounds like a picture book."

"I—I like yours," said Ermengarde.

Ermengarde tried hard as a student, but school did not come easily to her. "She must be *made* to learn," her father had told Miss Minchin. He did not understand how she could forget almost everything she learned.

"Would you like to come see Emily?" Sara asked.

"Who is Emily?" Ermengarde said.

"Come see," she replied.

"Is it true that you have your very own sitting room?" Ermengarde whispered as they walked along.

"Yes," said Sara. "I have my own space because I tell stories to myself and I don't want people to hear me."

"You make up stories?" gasped Ermengarde.

"Well, yes. Anyone can," replied Sara.

They had arrived at Sara's door. Sara whispered, "Let's be quiet and if we open the door suddenly, maybe we'll catch her."

There was a mysterious look in Sara's eye. Ermengarde had no idea what Sara meant, but she was excited anyway. Then Sara turned the handle and threw open the door.

"She returned to her chair before we could catch her!" said Sara.

Ermengarde looked at the doll and then at Sara. "Can she—walk?" she asked breathlessly.

"Yes, I believe she can," said Sara. "I pretend she can and that makes it seem true."

Ermengarde was so interested by this new girl that she stared at Sara instead of at Emily. The girls sat and talked for a while. Sara told Ermengarde about her life in Bombay and about the magic of dolls. When she talked about her father, a cloud seemed to pass over Sara's face and she looked quite sad.

"Are you in pain?" asked Ermengarde.

"Yes," said Sara, "but not in my body. I love my father more than anything else in the world, and now he is gone away." She put her head down on her knees for a moment and was quiet. "I promised him I would be brave, and I will."

Never in Ermengarde's life had she met anyone like Sara. When the lunch bell rang, she didn't want to leave. But before they went downstairs, they agreed to be best friends.

~ 4 ~
Lottie

Sara began to settle in at school. She was praised for how quickly she learned things, for her good manners, and for giving to the poor. Miss Minchin thought that if Sara were given many compliments and anything she wanted, Sara would stay.

She knew that if Sara wrote to her father that she was unhappy in any way, Captain Crewe would remove Sara from school at once. This would spoil most children. But not Sara.

She said to Ermengarde one day, "Nice things have happened to me by accident. It just happened that I always liked books and learning. I was born to a father who is nice and clever, and could give me anything. Maybe if something bad happened to me," said Sara, "I would not be such a nice child."

"But nothing bad has happened to Lavinia and she is not a nice girl," said Ermengarde.

Lavinia was, in fact, jealous of Sara. Until Sara's arrival, Lavinia had felt she was the star student. Lavinia was pretty and had been the best-dressed girl before Sara came in her velvet coats and fancy hats.

Sara had taken her place at the front of the line and Lavinia didn't like it. Unlike Lavinia, Sara was a leader because she was never mean or impolite to others.

"It's disgusting the way Miss Minchin shows off Sara when parents come," said Lavinia. " 'Dear Sara, please talk to Mrs. Musgrave about India,'" said Lavinia, speaking in a syrupy tone like Miss Minchin. " 'Sara must speak French to Lady Pitkin. Her accent is perfect,'" mimicked Lavinia again.

Sara was a friendly person who shared what she had with others, even the little ones. If a younger girl fell and scraped her knee, Sara ran to help her up and comforted her. Many older girls were not as nice to the little ones.

So the younger children adored Sara. Lottie Legh loved Sara so much she followed her around all day. Lottie was only four years old. When Lottie's mother had died, her father put her in school because he didn't know what else to do with her.

Since Lottie was born, she had been treated like a favorite pet. When she wanted something, she cried and screamed until she got it. Her crying would fill the house quite often.

One morning, Sara was walking by the sitting room when she heard Miss Amelia and Miss Minchin trying to calm Lottie.

"I don't have a maa-maa," wailed Lottie.

"Oh, Lottie!" yelled Miss Amelia. "Stop, darling! Please don't cry! Please don't."

Lottie wailed again.

"What a naughty child!" shouted Miss Minchin. "She should be punished!" Miss Minchin stood up and left the room.

When Miss Minchin reached the doorway, Sara said, "Perhaps I could make her quiet. May I try?"

"If you can," said Miss Minchin. And she walked off.

Then Miss Amelia got up and left with a heavy sigh, and little Lottie's pudgy legs kicked as hard as ever. Sara looked at the furious, howling child. After a few moments, Sara sat down next to Lottie and just waited.

Except for Lottie's angry screams, the room was quiet. Lottie was used to people pleading with her until she stopped crying. But now Lottie screamed and the only person in the room didn't care a bit. She opened her eyes to peek at Sara.

"I-don't-have-a-ma-ma," she announced.

Sara looked at her with kind eyes. "Neither do I," she said.

This was so unexpected that Lottie dropped her legs, lay quietly, and stared. She liked Sara.

"Where is she?" Lottie asked.

"She went to heaven," Sara explained. "But I am sure she comes to see me—though I don't see her. So does yours. Maybe they can both see us right now."

Lottie suddenly sat upright. If her mama had seen her temper tantrum maybe she would be ashamed of her.

Sara kept talking. She told Lottie of a heaven with fields of flowers, a soft wind, and little children running about. Lottie moved closer to Sara and drank in every word.

"I want to go there," said Lottie. "I don't have a mama in this school."

"I'll be your mama," Sara said.

"Really?" Lottie exclaimed.

"Yes," said Sara. "Let's go find Emily and tell her."

And the two girls trotted off hand in hand to Sara's room.

~ 5 ~

Becky

The schoolchildren loved to hear Sara tell stories. And Sara loved to tell them. One evening, Sara was in the corner of the schoolroom with a group of listeners when a servant girl dressed in dirty clothes came in the room. She had a heavy coal box that she set down by the fireplace. While she swept out the ashes, the girl appeared to be listening to Sara's story.

"The mermaids swam in the crystal green water," said Sara in a louder voice so the girl could hear. The girl became so interested that she stopped her work and sat down to listen. This was not allowed, but she had forgotten herself.

Sara talked on about strange sea flowers and faint music that could be heard under the sea. Suddenly the fireplace brush fell from the girl's hand and landed with a thud. Lavinia swirled around.

"That girl has been listening!" she cried.

The servant girl jumped up and dashed out of the room.

"I knew she was listening," said Sara. "Why shouldn't she?"

"I don't think your mama would want you telling stories to servant girls," said Lavinia. "*Mine* wouldn't."

"She wouldn't mind," said Sara. "My mother knew stories belong to everybody."

Sara marched out of the room, hoping she would see the servant girl in the hall, but she was not there.

That night Sara asked her maid, Mariette, who the girl was. Mariette told Sara she was a scullery maid. She polished boots, scrubbed floors, and was ordered around by everybody. She was a shy, sad little person who looked afraid when anyone spoke to her.

"What is her name?" asked Sara.

"Becky," replied Mariette. "I hear people yelling 'Becky do this,' 'Becky do that' all day long."

Sara tried to speak with Becky after that, but the girl hurried away whenever Sara saw her. A few weeks later, Sara came back to her room after dance class and found Becky asleep in her chair by the fire.

"Oh!" exclaimed Sara, surprised. "The poor thing!"

Becky had a black coal smudge on her nose and her hat was falling off her head. She had been cleaning the bedrooms and had sat down to rest a moment, and had fallen asleep from the fire's warmth.

Sara didn't want to wake Becky because she thought she worked too hard for a girl her age. But Sara knew Miss Minchin would be very angry if she discovered what Becky had done.

Just then Becky opened her eyes with a gasp and scrambled to her feet. "Oh—oh, miss. I'm sorry!" she said.

"Don't be afraid," said Sara. "You were tired. You could not help it." Sara laughed in a friendly way. Becky had never heard anyone laugh like that before. She was used to being yelled at and ordered around.

"We are really the same," said Sara. "I am a girl like you."

Becky's mouth hung open in disbelief. "Aren't you angry with me?" Becky asked. "Aren't you going to tell the missus?"

"No," cried Sara. "Of course not. Have you done your work? Maybe you could stay a bit. Would you like some cake?"

Becky felt as if she were in a dream. She never got enough to eat. After Becky gobbled down the cake, she and Sara talked by the fire.

"Becky," asked Sara, "you were listening to the story the other day, weren't you?"

"Yes, miss," admitted Becky. "I know I shouldn't have, but I couldn't help it."

"Would you like to hear the rest?" asked Sara.

"Oh, yes!" said Becky. "Could I?"

"We don't have time now, but when you clean the bedrooms again, I'll tell you part of it when you're done."

Becky smiled broadly. "I wouldn't mind the work at all if I had a story to think about."

When Becky went downstairs, she wasn't the same child. She had an extra piece of cake in her pocket, she had been fed and warmed, and she had made a friend.

~ 6 ~
Diamonds

Captain Crewe had written to Sara about a friend who had discovered diamonds on his land. The friend invited Captain Crewe to become his partner and to share his riches. Captain Crewe's letter was very exciting. It sounded like a fairy tale.

The girls at school talked and talked about the diamond mines and how rich Sara would be. Some were jealous of her.

"I don't believe in diamond mines." Lavinia snorted.

"Do you know what I've heard?" said Jessie with a giggle. "Sara likes to pretend she's a princess."

"Well, then," said Lavinia. "We should call her 'Your Royal Highness.'" The two girls laughed.

Just then Lottie and Sara came into the schoolroom. Classes were done for the day, and Miss Minchin left the girls alone during this time, but only if they were quiet.

Sara went to read by the window, and Lottie played with the little ones. As Lottie was running across the floor, she fell and cut her knee. She wailed loudly. Sara came to comfort her.

"Stop crying this minute!" yelled Lavinia. "Miss Minchin will hear you. I should shake you!"

Sara stood up quickly. "Well," Sara said to Lavinia, "I would like to shake you, but I won't. We are both old enough to know better."

"Yes, Your Royal Highness," Lavinia said with a smirk. "The school is quite fashionable now that it has a princess."

Sara was furious. She was sensitive about her latest "pretend" about being a princess and she wished it to be a secret. But now Lavinia was telling the whole school.

Sara's face became hot and she almost flew at Lavinia in anger. But she stopped herself. A princess did not lose her temper. "It's true I pretend I am a princess sometimes. I do it so I can try to behave like one."

Lavinia could not think of a thing to say. She and Jessie just walked away.

To Becky, Sara did seem like a princess. She was very kind to Becky and told her stories when Becky finished her work. Sara always gave Becky something to eat, and soon Becky lost her hungry, tired feeling. Sara had no idea how her stories and laughter fed Becky, too.

A few weeks before Sara's eleventh birthday, a letter came from her father in India. Captain Crewe was feeling sick and was having trouble with the diamond mines. He wrote that he would feel so much better if his "Little Missus" were there.

Captain Crewe had made many plans for Sara's birthday. He ordered a new doll with lots of beautiful fancy clothes. Sara wrote back to her father that she would enjoy it very much, but that this would be her last doll, as she was getting too old.

When Captain Crewe received Sara's letter, he laughed harder than he had in weeks. He wanted only to be with Sara that very minute.

Sara's birthday party was all planned. The schoolroom was to be decorated, and there was going to be a feast in Miss Minchin's room. That morning Sara found a present in her room: a shabby red flannel pincushion that Becky had made for her.

"It's nothing but flannel," Becky said, "and it ain't new, but I wanted to give you something. I thought you might be able to pretend it was made of real satin with diamond pins in it."

Sara ran to Becky and hugged her.

"Thank you, thank you, Becky!" Sara said.

~ 7 ~

Everything Changes

Sara entered the party room walking next to Miss Minchin. The servants stood in a line behind them, carrying all of the presents. At the end of the line, Becky carried the final gift. This is how Miss Minchin wanted the party to start.

"You may leave," Miss Minchin said to the servants with a wave of her hand.

"Can Becky stay?" asked Sara.

"Becky?" Miss Minchin said with disbelief. "Becky is a scullery maid."

"But she is a little girl, too," said Sara. "Please let her stay."

Miss Minchin replied carefully. "Because you ask as a birthday favor, she may stay. Becky, thank Miss Sara for her great kindness."

Becky curtsied to Sara several times. They gave each other a look of understanding. "Thank you, miss!" Becky said.

"Go stand over there," said Miss Minchin without a smile. "Not too close to the young ladies."

Becky didn't care where she stood, as long as she was allowed to stay.

Miss Minchin cleared her throat and began to make a speech. Sara became very uncomfortable.

"Dear Sara is eleven years old today," she started.

"*Dear* Sara," complained Lavinia to the girl beside her.

"She is not like other little girls. Sara will have a large fortune some day. Her schooling will help her with that fortune. Sara's French and her dancing are important for the school. Her manners—for which you call her 'Princess Sara'—are perfect. Please thank Sara for inviting you to her party."

All the children stood and said, "Thank you, Sara!"

"Thank you for coming," replied Sara.

After Miss Minchin left the room, the girls rushed toward the presents. Sara opened the box with the Last Doll. When the doll's trunk full of clothes was opened, the children all talked excitedly.

Suddenly Miss Amelia came into the room. "Sara, Miss Minchin has an important visitor and needs this room for her meeting. Please go to the parlor for the feast now. Becky, you must go back to work."

Becky began to pick up things from the floor until she heard Miss Minchin coming down the hall. She was so afraid of being caught in the party room that she crawled under the table to hide.

Miss Minchin entered the room and sat down with a worried-looking man.

"Mr. Barrow," Miss Minchin started, "I understand that you are Captain Crewe's lawyer. What would you like to speak with me about?"

The man looked around at the Last Doll and all of the gifts. "Captain Crewe spent too much money on his daughter," he exclaimed.

"Captain Crewe is a very rich man, Mr. Barrow," said Miss Minchin. "I think he can spend his money how he wants. The diamond mines alone would—"

But Mr. Barrow cut her off. "The diamond mines! There are none!" said Mr. Barrow.

"What!" cried Miss Minchin. "What do you mean?"

"His dear friend's diamond mines did not have diamonds after all," said Mr. Barrow. "And now all of his money is gone and Captain Crewe is, too."

"Gone?" Miss Minchin cried out. "How can he be gone?"

"He's dead, ma'am," Mr. Barrow answered. "He died of jungle fever and worrying about his business troubles. His friend ran away with what money was left. The shock was too much for Captain Crewe."

Now Miss Minchin understood. She had never

received such bad news in her life. Her show student and her money were being taken away from her. She felt as if she were being robbed.

"Sara is left a beggar?" she exclaimed.

"Yes," said Mr. Barrow. "And she is left to you. She has no relatives that we know of."

With that Miss Minchin almost exploded. She could hear the happy and expensive party going on in the next room.

"At this moment Sara is sitting in my room wearing a fancy dress and giving a party with my money!" she almost screamed.

"I am not responsible for any of this," Mr. Barrow said. "Captain Crewe did not pay our last bill, either."

"I've paid for all of her clothes, the French maid, the carriage, and the pony—all of it since the last check came from Captain Crewe. What am I to do?"

"You are now responsible for Sara," he explained again.

"No!" yelled Miss Minchin. "I will put her out on the street!"

"I wouldn't do that," said Mr. Barrow carefully. "You and the school would not look good. A teacher putting a girl out on the street with no money or friends? You'd better keep her and make use of her."

At that Mr. Barrow tipped his hat at Miss Minchin. "Good-bye," he said, and walked out.

Miss Minchin stood there, breathless, not able to say a word. Just then Miss Amelia came through the door.

"Where is Sara Crewe?" bellowed Miss Minchin.

Miss Amelia was frightened by her sister. "She's—she's with the others," she stammered.

"Have her put on a black dress immediately and take off that silly pink party dress right now! No more fancy clothes!"

"Oh, sister," said Amelia shakily. "What happened?"

In an angry, bitter voice Miss Minchin told her sister about Captain Crewe. Then she told Miss Amelia to go and tell Sara. Miss Amelia left with hunched shoulders to do as she was told.

As Miss Minchin turned to leave the room, she heard a loud sob. "What is that?" she said angrily. When she heard it again, she lifted up the tablecloth and found Becky under the table, crying.

"How dare you?" she cried. "Come out right now!"

Poor Becky crawled out with a tear-stained face. "I didn't mean to listen. I was scared when you came in and I slipped under the table. I'm—I'm so sorry for Miss Sara!"

"Leave the room!" boomed Miss Minchin.

Becky ran out the door as fast as she could.

8

A New Life

When Miss Amelia told Sara her father had died and his fortune was lost, Sara did not say a word. Her eyes got bigger and bigger and then she ran upstairs to her room. Unlike Sara, several other children began to cry when they heard the news.

Sara was called to Miss Minchin's room. Even by that time, the birthday party seemed as if it had been a dream. Every sign of the party had been taken away. When Sara arrived she looked pale and had dark circles under her eyes. She was wearing the black dress, which was much too small for her.

"Everything will be different now," began Miss Minchin coldly. "I hope Miss Amelia has explained it to you."

"Yes, my papa is dead and I am quite poor," said Sara quietly.

"You are a beggar," said Miss Minchin. "It seems you have no family and no one to take care of you."

Sara stood silently, looking straight ahead.

"What are you staring at?" demanded Miss

Minchin. "Don't you understand? You are alone in the world unless I keep you out of charity."

"I understand," Sara answered. She gulped hard and tried not to cry.

"You are not a princess any more. Your carriage, your pony, and your maid will be sent away. You will wear your oldest and plainest clothes. You will be like Becky. You must work for your living."

Sara looked brighter. "If I can work it will not matter so much."

"If you make yourself useful, I may let you stay here," said Miss Minchin sternly. "If you don't please me, you will be sent away. Remember that."

Sara stood still a moment, thinking about what had been said and then she turned to go.

"Stop!" ordered Miss Minchin. "Aren't you going to thank me?"

"What for?" asked Sara.

"For my kindness in giving you a home," said Miss Minchin.

Sara took two steps forward. In a fierce, low tone she answered, "You are not kind. And this is *not* a home." She turned to run out of the room before Miss Minchin could stop her.

Sara ran upstairs toward her room. But as she reached the door, Miss Amelia came out of it looking nervous. The truth was, Miss Amelia was ashamed of what she was about to do.

"You are not to go in there," Miss Amelia said quietly. "It is no longer your room."

"Then where is my room?" asked Sara.

"You are to sleep in the attic with Becky."

Becky had told Sara where she lived. Sara turned and walked up two flights of stairs. As she opened the attic door, her heart gave a thump. The paint was peeling off the walls. There was a rusty grate covering the fireplace and a worn blanket covering a hard bed. Under the skylight in the roof was an old stool. Sara went to sit on it. She rarely cried and she did not cry now.

Sara laid Emily across her knees and put her face down on the doll. She sat for a while like this until she heard a tap at the door. Becky's tear-smeared face peeked in.

"Oh, miss, may I—may I come in?" asked Becky.

Sara lifted her head and tried to smile, but could not. Suddenly she held out her hand to Becky and gave a little sob.

"Oh, Becky," she said. "I told you we were just the same, just two little girls. There's no difference now. I'm not a princess anymore."

Becky ran to Sara and held her hand.

"Yes, miss, you are," Becky cried. "Whatever happens to you, you'll always be a princess."

~ 9 ~

The Attic

The first night Sara spent in the attic was a night she never forgot. She could think of only one thing.

"My papa is dead!" she kept whispering to herself.

It wasn't until much later that she realized how hard her bed was and how much the wind howled in the attic. And there was something worse: the shuffling and squeaking in the walls. Becky had told her it was the sound of rats. Sara even heard them scurry across the floor. She sat up in bed trembling.

The change in her life came all at once, and it was hard to get used to. Mariette had left the house. When Sara went down to breakfast, her seat next to Miss Minchin was now occupied by Lavinia. Sara was told to sit instead with the little children and help them.

Sara had many jobs. She taught the younger children French and she went on errands. The cook and the maids enjoyed ordering Sara around, and they often blamed her for things that went wrong.

Sara's own schoolwork stopped. But after a long day of hard work, she was allowed to study alone at night.

One of the strangest changes for Sara was that she could no longer talk to the other schoolchildren. It was clear Miss Minchin wanted her to stay away from them. Sara's dresses became smaller and shabbier, and her shoes were filled with holes. She began to look strange. Soon she was told to eat separately from the schoolchildren.

Sara never told anyone how she felt about these changes. "Soldiers don't complain," she would say. But there were times when her heart would have broken if she did not have three people in her life: Becky, Ermengarde, and Lottie.

Throughout every night, Sara felt better knowing that Becky was on the other side of the wall. Becky was very kind to her. Before sunrise, she would come to her room and help Sara dress.

As for Ermengarde, she remained Sara's friend, unlike the other girls at school. In the beginning, Sara and Ermengarde both thought the other did not want to be friends anymore. They did not see or speak to each other for a long time.

But late one night, as Sara walked up to the attic, she saw a light under her door. *That's strange*, she thought, *no one comes up here but me.*

When she opened the door, she found Ermengarde sitting on the footstool. She was in her nightgown and her eyes were red from crying. "I know I could get in trouble," Ermengarde said. "But I don't care. I need to know why you don't like me anymore."

"But I do like you," Sara said. "All of the other girls don't want to talk to me anymore. So I thought you didn't, either."

"Oh, Sara," she wailed. And she rushed into Sara's arms. "I couldn't bear it anymore, so tonight I decided to come up and talk to you."

"I'm so glad you did," said Sara.

Ermengarde looked slowly around the attic. "Do you think you can stand living here, Sara?"

"I can if I pretend it's a different place," she answered. "People have lived in worse places. I can pretend I'm a prisoner." Sara's eyes flashed with an idea, and she looked like her old self again. "Miss Minchin is the jailer, and Becky is the prisoner in the next cell! If I pretend this, it will make me feel much better."

"If I come up at night," asked Ermengarde, "will you tell me what you've made up that day? We could be best friends again."

"Yes," replied Sara. "Hard times prove how good your friends are."

~ 10 ~
A Rat

Little Lottie was confused about the changes she noticed in Sara. The older girl looked very different, and Lottie had heard people whispering about Sara living in another room.

So late one afternoon, Lottie went on her own to find Sara's room. Finally, she reached the attic and pushed open one of the doors. Sara was standing on the stool looking out the attic window.

"Mama Sara!" cried Lottie. She was surprised that the attic was so bare and ugly.

Sara jumped down from her stool and ran over to Lottie. "Don't make any noise," she said. "If anyone hears us, we will be in trouble. And I've been yelled at enough today." Then she said quietly, "It's not such a bad room."

"It isn't?" asked Lottie in a whisper.

Sara hugged her and tried to laugh. "You can see all kinds of things from this window that you can't see downstairs," she said.

"Like what?" Lottie asked.

"Chimneys," Sara answered, "with smoke curling

out of them, and other windows with heads peeking out. You can wonder who they are. It's a different world up here."

Sara lifted Lottie up to see the sparrows hopping around the rooftop. The sky seemed much closer than when you saw it from the street.

"Oh, Sara," cried Lottie. "I like it up here. I think it's even nicer than downstairs."

Sara smiled at her.

When the girls looked around the room again, Sara told Lottie what she imagined the room looked like. From this day on, it became a ritual Sara liked to say aloud to make herself feel better. "There is a thick blue Indian rug on the floor. In that corner, there's a soft little sofa with a shelf full of books, and a rug in front of the fireplace. On the walls, there are hanging pictures, and there is a table with a lamp on it. And the bed is soft with a lovely silk cover."

"Oh, Sara," cried Lottie, imagining it all, "I would love to live here, too."

Soon Lottie knew it was time say good-bye to Sara. When Lottie had gone, Sara looked around the dark room with bare floors and broken furniture. She felt worse than before Lottie had come. Her dreams about the room melted away. Sara hung her head.

Then she heard a little noise and looked up. A large rat was sitting on the floor in front of her, sniffing for the bread crumbs that were on the floor near Sara.

The rat looked at her carefully with bright eyes.

"It must be hard to be a rat," Sara said to him. "Nobody likes you."

The rat moved closer to the crumbs as Sara talked. He was very hungry and had a family to feed.

"Go ahead," said Sara. "I won't hurt you. I'll be your friend."

Somehow the rat knew that he was safe with Sara. He stepped slowly toward the crumbs and began to eat. The largest crumb he saved for last. When Sara sat very still, the rat grabbed the big crumb and hurried to his hole in the wall.

And from that day on, Sara had a new friend in the attic.

~ 11 ~

The Indian Gentleman

Even though Sara had her friends, she was still lonely. It was dangerous for Lottie and Ermengarde to visit Sara because Miss Amelia sometimes checked on the girls in bed. So they couldn't visit Sara often.

In the evening Sara could see into the windows of the homes around the school. There was a family of eight children she called the Large Family. They would go for walks with their nurses, ride in their carriage, and cheer when their father came home at night.

Sara was walking by their house one evening as the children were getting into a carriage. The little boy about five years old had rosy cheeks and blue eyes. Sara couldn't help but stand and look.

It was Christmastime and the children had been learning about giving to the poor. The boy had a coin he wanted to give Sara. She looked shabby and thin, and her eyes appeared hungry.

"Here, poor little girl," he said, handing her the coin.

Sara remembered the poor children who used to

stare at her when she got out of her carriage. Her face went pale.

"Oh, no," she said. "No, thank you. I must not take it!"

Her voice was so unlike an ordinary street child's voice and her manners were so polite that the other children turned to listen.

"Yes, you must," said the boy. "You can buy food with it."

The boy's face looked so kind that Sara thought he would be disappointed if she did not take the coin. So she did.

"Thank you," said Sara. "You are a kind little darling."

Before now, Sara knew she looked shabby, but she did not know she looked like a beggar. Now she knew.

The children in the carriage talked with excitement about Sara. "She didn't talk like a beggar!" said one of the older girls.

"She said 'thank you' in a very grand way," said the boy.

And from that moment on, the Large Family called Sara "the-girl-who-is-not-a-beggar." They would watch Sara as she walked by on the street. Sara knew nothing about this. All she knew was that her feelings for the Large Family got stronger. She wore the coin on a chain around her neck and thought of them often.

Sara tried to think of the good things in her sad life. She loved Becky more and more each day for being a good friend. She enjoyed teaching the little girls' French class. The young students loved her and tried to stand near her.

Sara made friends with the sparrows on the rooftop. And she often talked to the rat. But she was still lonely. It would be so nice if someone moved in to the attic of the house next door, she thought.

The next day, as if her dreams were answered, she saw a van full of furniture being unloaded in front of the house next door. On the sidewalk Sara saw furniture that looked like things she had had in India. She felt as if the new neighbors were already her friends.

At night, Becky would visit Sara and bring her news. "The man next door is a rich Indian," Becky said. "He's sick, though, and the man from the Large Family is his lawyer."

One day a carriage pulled up to the house with the father of the Large Family, a nurse, and two servants. They brought out the Indian man, who looked very sick, and then they all went into the house. A little later a doctor came.

This was the beginning of the story of the Indian gentleman.

~ 12 ~
Ram Dass

Sunsets outside the attic window were pink with piles of red and gold clouds. On the street level you could see none of this. When it was possible to leave the kitchen without being missed, Sara would run upstairs to see the sunsets.

One evening as she was looking out, Sara heard a sound from the window of the next attic. A dark-faced man with a white turban on his head was peeking out of the skylight. He was an Indian manservant, a *lascar*. The man was holding a small monkey.

Sara thought how homesick she was when she looked at the dark-faced man. She smiled at him across the rooftop.

Sara's smile brightened the man's face. But when he waved at her, the monkey got loose and ran across the roof. It jumped on Sara's shoulder and then into her room!

Sara laughed. She turned to the *lascar* and spoke in the Hindustani language she had learned in India. "Will he let me catch him?" she asked.

Sara could see the man was surprised that she

knew his language. He spoke politely to her and called himself Ram Dass. He said the monkey was difficult to catch. Ram Dass asked if he could come get him.

"Yes, come," said Sara.

Ram Dass crossed the roof quickly and slipped through Sara's window. He turned to Sara and bowed to her in thanks. Then he chased after the little monkey until he caught it.

Ram Dass thanked Sara several times. He noticed the shabbiness of the room, but he spoke to Sara as if she were the daughter of a queen. Ram Dass said the monkey belonged to his sick master, and he would be sad if the monkey were lost. Then he bowed once more to Sara and walked back over the rooftop with ease.

Sara felt homesick for India and her life with her father. She knew the best future she could hope for would be to become a teacher at Miss Minchin's school—and to follow her every rule. *Whatever happens*, thought Sara, *I will act like a princess*.

So even when the servants or Miss Minchin were rude and ordered her about, Sara was polite. Sara never forgot to say please or thank you, even to those who were not kind to her.

The morning after she met Ram Dass, Sara was in the schoolroom with Miss Minchin and her young

41

students. She was thinking of how funny it would be if Miss Minchin discovered she was a real princess. Sara, with her toes sticking out of her shoes! She smiled and had a look in her eyes that Miss Minchin hated.

When Miss Minchin saw her, she flew over to Sara and grabbed her by the shoulders. Sara was so surprised that she pulled back from Miss Minchin and let out a chuckle.

"What is so funny?" Miss Minchin yelled.

"I was just thinking," said Sara.

"Say you are sorry immediately!" replied Miss Minchin.

"I will apologize for laughing," Sara said, "but not for thinking."

"What were you thinking?" she demanded.

Lavinia and Jessie whispered to each other. They were always interested when Miss Minchin got angry with Sara because Sara never seemed to be afraid of her.

"I was thinking," Sara said, "that you would not treat me this way if I were a princess. How surprised and frightened you would be if you found out that I was one!"

Every pair of eyes in the room widened.

"Go to your room!" cried Miss Minchin breathlessly.

Sara made a little bow and left Miss Minchin.

The schoolgirls whispered excitedly. "I wouldn't be surprised if she did turn out to be a princess," they said.

~ 13 ~

The Other Side
of the Wall

Sara liked the Large Family because they looked happy. And she liked the Indian gentleman because he looked unhappy.

The cook in the kitchen had heard that the Indian gentleman was actually an Englishman who had lived in India. His name was Mr. Carrisford. He had gotten news that his fortune was going to be lost. The news so upset him that he got sick and almost died. Mr. Carrisford still was not well, though his fortune was returned. The troublesome business he had been in was diamond mines.

After hearing this, Sara felt closer to Mr. Carrisford. He had had the same troubles as her papa. At night Sara would stop and look in the windows at him. He often looked into the fire gloomily.

The father of the Large Family would frequently visit the man next door with his oldest daughters, Janet and Nora. During one of these visits, Janet told Mr. Carrisford about the-girl-who-was-not-a-beggar.

He was very interested, especially when he heard Ram Dass tell about the adventure with the monkey.

"Carmichael," Mr. Carrisford said to the father of the Large Family, "I wonder how many little servant girls are in uncomfortable attics around this square. Do you think the girl I'm searching for could be a servant now, too?"

Mr. Carmichael knew worrying was the worst thing for the Indian gentleman's health. "If the child from the Paris school is the one you are looking for," Mr. Carmichael said, "we know she is being cared for by adoptive parents from Russia."

"So we are not sure if this is the right child?" asked Mr. Carrisford.

"Correct," said Mr. Carmichael. "But the girl's story is the same: An English officer in India put his little girl in school. He died suddenly after losing his fortune."

"I wish I knew more about her," said the Indian gentleman.

"But do you think she went to Paris?" asked Mr. Carmichael.

"Perhaps," replied Mr. Carrisford. "Her mother was a Frenchwoman." Then he leaned forward and slapped his hand on the table. "We must find her, Carmichael," he said. "If she is alive, she is without a friend or money and it is all my fault."

"Try to calm down," said Mr. Carmichael. "Remember that when you find her, you have a fortune to give to her."

"Poor Crewe trusted me. And he died thinking I had ruined him," the Indian gentleman said.

"Please don't feel guilty," said Mr. Carmichael.

"I am guilty," he replied. "I am guilty of not facing my friend to tell him I had ruined his fortune for him and his child."

Mr. Carmichael put a hand on the Indian man's shoulder. "You ran away because you had brain fever. Do not forget you were in the hospital two days later and could not think or speak because you were so sick."

"Yes," said Mr. Carrisford. "And when I returned from the hospital, Crewe was dead."

"Do you think you heard Captain Crewe say her name?" asked Mr. Carmichael.

"I don't know," he replied. "But he called her by a nickname, 'Little Missus.'"

"We will find her," said Mr. Carmichael. "I will go to Moscow to search for the Russian parents."

"Thank you for helping me," Mr. Carrisford said as he took his hand. "Thank you."

~ ~ ~

At that very moment, on the other side of the wall, Sara sat talking to the rat.

"It was hard to be a princess today," she said. "Lavinia laughed at my muddy skirt and I wanted to snap at her. But you can't do that when you are a princess."

"Oh, Papa," Sara said sadly, putting her head in her hands. "It seems such a long time since I was your 'Little Missus!'"

~ 14 ~

A Hungry Child

O ne cold and dark winter day, it had rained endlessly. The streets were filled with sloppy mud. Though her clothes were wet through and her shoes could hold no more water, Sara was sent out again and again on errands. She had not eaten all that day or the night before.

Sara hurried along the streets and tried to think of something else. *I will pretend I have dry clothes on*, Sara thought. *And a long wool coat and dry shoes. And I will pretend I have found a coin on the street. I will buy six hot buns with it.*

Just then Sara looked down and saw a silver coin lying in the gutter! A fourpence. "Oh, it's true!" gasped Sara. When she looked up, she found she was standing in front of a bakery. Inside a woman was putting a tray of hot buns in the window. Sara could hardly believe her eyes. The magic was at work!

As she climbed the stairs to the bakery, Sara saw a beggar girl dressed in rags and huddling in the corner. She had muddy toes sticking out of her shoes.

Tangled hair covered her dirty face.

"When did you last eat?" Sara asked the girl.

"Don't know," she replied in a hoarse voice.

Sara knew the girl was hungrier than she was. She knew that a princess would share what she had. So Sara went into the shop.

"Have you lost a fourpence?" she asked the baker.

"No," the woman said. "Did you find it?"

"Yes," Sara said. "In the gutter."

"Keep it then," the woman said. "It could have been there a week. We won't find the owner now. Want to buy something?"

"Four buns please," said Sara. Her stomach growled. Sara saw that the baker put in six.

"Just four please," she said again. "I only have a fourpence."

"I'll put in two more anyway," the woman replied. Sara thanked the baker for her kindness and left the shop. On the steps, she opened her bag and gave the beggar girl one of the hot buns.

The child stared in disbelief at the bun in her hand. Then she crammed it into her mouth. Sara took out three more buns and put them in the girl's lap.

She is starving, thought Sara. *But I'm not starving, I'm only hungry*. Sara bent down and put the fifth bun in the girl's lap.

The child was still stuffing the buns in her mouth when Sara walked away. Then the baker woman looked out of her window. "Well, I don't believe it!" said the woman. "That girl gave her buns to the beggar child. And she was so hungry herself."

The baker went outside and spoke to the child with a worried face. "Come inside," she said. "And get yourself warm by the fire. Whenever you need a little bread, just come here and ask for it." Sara walked along the street. She was pleased to have her one bun. She broke it into little pieces and tried to make it last.

As she passed the Large Family's home, she could see that the father was going on a trip. Sara stood outside the window a moment. The father was kissing each child. *Oh, how they will miss him! thought Sara. I will miss him, too, even though he doesn't know me.*

The door opened and Sara moved off to the side so that she would not be seen. The children were wishing their father a good trip. "If you find the little girl in Moscow," said the youngest boy, "give her our love."

The father got into the carriage and drove away.

"Did you see," said Janet to Nora inside the house, "the-little-girl-who-is-not-a-beggar? She was

50

cold and wet. The people at the school send her out in terrible weather."

Meanwhile, Sara was climbing the stairs and thinking, *I wonder who the little girl is—the girl he is looking for?*

~ 15 ~

Visitors in the Attic

On the afternoon Sara was out, a strange thing happened in the attic. The rat was the only one to see it.

A sound came from the roof. The skylight opened and two men climbed in the window: Ram Dass and another man, who was Mr. Carrisford's secretary.

The secretary spotted the rat as he scurried in his hole. "Was that a rat?" he asked Ram Dass in a whisper.

"Yes," he answered. "There are many in the walls."

"The child must be scared of them," the secretary said.

"She is not like other children," Ram Dass said. "I watch her from the roof sometimes to see that she is safe. The sparrows come to her. She feeds the rat and talks to him."

"Are you sure no one will come up here and surprise us?" asked the secretary. "Then Mr. Carrisford's plan would be ruined."

"No," said Ram Dass. "No one comes up here but her."

The secretary took out a pencil and paper and began writing notes. First he went to the bed and felt it. "Hard as stone," he said. "That will have to be fixed another day. It can't be done tonight."

He lifted the blanket. "Blanket dingy and worn, sheets have holes," the secretary said aloud. "What a bed for a child!"

He moved to the fireplace. It had not been lit for a long time. "Who made this plan?" he asked.

"I first thought of it," said Ram Dass. "I like the child and we are both lonely. I have heard her say many times how she pretends she has nice things in this room. Her face lights up when she speaks of it.

"When Mr. Carrisford was feeling ill, I told him about her," Ram Dass continued. "He wanted to make her dreams real."

"Do you think we can do all of this while she sleeps?" asked the secretary.

"I can move with silent feet," replied Ram Dass. "When she does wake, she will think a magician has been here."

"I think I've made enough notes. We can go now," said the secretary. Then he thought a moment. "Mr. Carrisford has a warm heart. It is a terrible thing that he has not found the lost child."

"If he does find her, I know he will get well," said Ram Dass.

~ 16 ~

Ermengarde's Gift

When Sara returned to the house, Miss Minchin was angry with her for being late. The cook was angry with her, too.

"May I have something to eat?" Sara asked quietly.

"Tea's done with," said the cook.

"But I had no dinner," Sara said in a low voice.

"There's some bread in the pantry," said the cook. "That's all you get this time of day."

The bread was old and dry, but it was all she had. Sara climbed the stairs slowly because she was so tired and hungry. When reached the top, she saw a light under the door. Ermengarde had come for a visit. She would brighten the room a little.

"Sara," exclaimed Ermengarde when Sara opened the door, "I am so glad you've come. But you do look tired."

"I am," said Sara.

"Papa sent me some books," said Ermengarde.

Sara ran over to the pile of books and picked up the top one. "Oh, *French Revolution*! I've wanted to read this!" said Sara.

"I haven't," said Ermengarde. "And Papa will be angry if I don't. What should I do?"

"I can read the books and tell you what's in them," said Sara.

"Do you think that will work?" Ermengarde asked.

"The little girls always remember what I tell them because I make it interesting," said Sara. "Maybe you will, too."

Ermengarde smiled widely at Sara. She could hardly believe her luck in finding such a wonderful friend.

Then they heard the sound of Miss Minchin's angry voice on the stairs below. Sara sprang off the bed and put out her candle.

"She is yelling at Becky," she whispered.

"Will she come up here?" asked Ermengarde.

"No," Sara said. "She will think I'm in bed. Don't move."

"You horrible lying child!" they heard Miss Minchin yell. "Eating half a meat pie—indeed!"

"'Twasn't me," sobbed Becky. "I was hungry, but it 'twasn't me. I could have eaten a whole one."

"Don't lie," said Miss Minchin. "Go to your room!"

They heard Becky run to her room and close the door, sobbing all the way.

"'Twas cook gave it to her policeman," Becky cried.

Sara was standing in the darkness clenching her fists.

"The awful mean thing!" she burst out. "The cook takes things and says Becky steals them. She doesn't! She's so hungry sometimes, she eats crusts from the garbage!"

Sara burst into tears. Ermengarde had never seen Sara cry. Suppose . . . A new thought entered Ermengarde's head.

"Sara," she asked in a quiet, scared voice, "you never told me—are—are you ever hungry?"

"Yes," Sara said in a gush. "Yes, I am. I'm so hungry now I could eat you. It's worse for Becky. She's hungrier than I am."

Ermengarde gasped. "Oh," she said. "I never knew."

"I didn't want you to know. It would make me feel like a beggar."

Ermengarde jumped back. What Sara said made her think of a wonderful idea. "Oh, Sara!" she said. "How silly I had not thought of this before!"

"What is it?" asked Sara.

"This afternoon my aunt sent me a big box full of good things. I didn't touch it because I ate too much at dinner. It's got cake in it, and meat pies, and jam and buns, oranges and chocolate. I'll creep back to my room and we'll eat it now."

Sara almost fell backwards. She grabbed Ermengarde's arm.

"Do you think you could?"

"Yes, of course," said Ermengarde. "The lights are out and everyone is in bed."

"Oh, Ermengarde," said Sara with excitement. "Let's pretend it's a party! And let's invite the prisoner in the next room."

"Yes," said Ermengarde. "Knock for Becky on the wall now and I'll go get the basket."

~ 17 ~

The Party

"**M**iss Ermengarde," said Sara, "is bring-
ing a box of good things to us."
Becky's cap almost fell off. "Good
things to eat, miss?" asked Becky hopefully.

"Yes," said Sara, "and we are going to have a
party."

"Oh, miss!" said Becky. "I know it was you who
asked her to let me come. Thank you, thank you!"

"Something good always happens," said Sara,
"before things get too bad. I need to remember that.
It's almost like magic."

Sara had a twinkle in her eye. "Now let's set the
table!"

"With what?" asked Becky.

Sara looked around and saw Ermengarde's red
shawl. "We can use this as a tablecloth," she said
happily. "Now what else?"

Sara thought for a moment and then ran over to
her old trunk in the corner of the room. There was
nothing but trash left in it, but she knew she could
find something. She saw a bunch of small white

handkerchiefs. "These are the plates," she said. "Golden plates."

Sara pulled out an old hat with a wreath of flowers on it. She took the flowers off and put them on the table. "These are flower garlands for the feast," she said. Then she placed the candlestick in the center of the table and stood back.

Becky looked at the table. "My, ain't it lovely!" she whispered.

"We're in a banquet hall," said Sara. "There are musicians playing in the corner and a fireplace with a huge fire in it."

"I can see it, miss!" Becky said in a whisper.

Then the door opened and Ermengarde came in. She could hardly carry the heavy basket of food in her arms. She looked at the beautiful table. "Oh, Sara!" Ermengarde cried. "You are the most clever girl."

"It's like a queen's table," said Becky.

"Let's pretend that this is a royal feast," said Ermengarde, "and, Sara, you are the princess."

"But it's your feast, Ermengarde," said Sara. "We can be your maids of honor."

"Oh, no," said Ermengarde, "you be the princess, Sara."

"Okay," Sara replied. "If you want me to." Sara led the way to the table. They had barely had time to put a piece of cake in their mouths when they heard footsteps.

Someone was coming up the stairs!

"It's Miss Minchin!" cried Becky, dropping her piece of cake on the floor.

Sara's eyes looked scared and large on her small white face.

Miss Minchin opened the door with the smack of her hand. She was pale with anger as she looked around the room.

"Lavinia was telling the truth," said Miss Minchin.

She went over to Becky and shook her. "You terrible child. You must leave the house in the morning!"

Sara stood in shock. Ermengarde began to cry.

"Don't send her away," Ermengarde said. "My aunt sent me the basket. We were just having a party."

"So I see," said Miss Minchin. "With Princess Sara sitting at the head of the table."

She turned to Sara. "I know you did this," she said fiercely. "You will not have anything to eat all day tomorrow."

"I did not have anything to eat today," said Sara quietly.

"All the better," said Miss Minchin. "Then you

will have something to remember."

"Go to your attic," Miss Minchin said to Becky.

Becky put her face in her apron. She left the room, her shoulders shaking.

"And you—" Miss Minchin said to Ermengarde, "you brought your beautiful new books to this dirty attic. What would your father say if he knew where you were tonight?"

Miss Minchin looked at Sara. She had a serious look on her face. "Why do you look at me like that?" asked Miss Minchin.

"I was wondering," said Sara.

"Wondering what?" asked Miss Minchin angrily.

"I was wondering," she said in a low voice, "what my father would say if he knew where I am tonight."

Miss Minchin ran to Sara and shook her shoulders now.

"How dare you!" she yelled. Then Miss Minchin stepped back. She picked up the books and the basket of food and pushed Ermengarde through the doorway.

Sara's dream was at an end. The table was bare. There were no golden plates. The flowers were trampled on the floor. Sara hung her head. But if she had glanced at the skylight instead, she would have seen Ram Dass.

Then Sara crawled slowly into bed and fell asleep.

~ ~ ~

She did not know how long she slept, but Sara knew she slept soundly. Strangely enough, Sara felt too warm and comfortable to open her eyes right away. She thought she was dreaming.

She felt a soft warm quilt around her and heard a crackling noise. When she opened her eyes to see what it was, she smiled. *I must still be dreaming,* she thought. *For this cannot be true!*

In the fireplace there was a blazing fire. On the floor was a thick red rug. A chair with cushions was in front of the fire. A table with small covered dishes of food was next to it. On the bed were new blankets and a silk robe. There were soft, warm slippers and even a stack of new books.

Oh, I've never had such a wonderful dream, thought Sara. She got out of bed and felt the rug on her feet.

"I am dreaming, but it feels real," she said aloud. She went to the fire and felt its heat. She pulled away in surprise.

"A fire I dreamed about wouldn't be *hot*!" she cried.

She jumped up and touched the table, the dishes, and the rug. She touched the blankets on the bed and the silk robe. "It's soft. It's warm. It must be real!" Sara cried. "I'm *not* dreaming!"

She almost tripped on her way over to the books. When she opened the one on top, Sara saw something was written inside. It said: "To the little girl in the attic. From a friend."

Sara began to cry with happiness. "I don't know who it is," she said. "But somebody cares about me. I have a friend."

She took the candle and went to Becky's room. "Becky!" Sara cried. "Wake up! You must come see."

Becky awoke and saw Sara dressed in the silk robe. She saw the Sara she remembered—Princess Sara. When the door of Sara's room was closed behind them, Becky stood in the warm glow of the fire with her mouth open. She could not speak.

"It's all real!" said Sara. "I've touched everything and it is real. The magic came while we were sleeping."

~ 18 ~
The Magic

Sara and Becky sat by the warm fire and opened the covered dishes. There was rich hot soup, sandwiches, toast, and muffins. The girls ate until their stomachs were full.

"I don't know who could have done all this," Sara said.

"Do you think it could melt away?" whispered Becky. "Maybe we should eat fast." She crammed a muffin in her mouth.

"No," said Sara. "I can taste this muffin. You never actually taste things in dreams. And I keep giving myself pinches. It's real."

The girls felt sleepy and comfortable. It was a feeling of happy, well-fed children. Sara looked over at her bed longingly. She even had enough blankets to share with Becky.

As Becky left that night, she looked at Sara with a big smile.

"If it ain't here in the mornin', I'll never forget it."

~ ~ ~

The next morning everyone in the school knew that Sara was in very serious trouble with Miss Minchin. They also knew that Ermengarde was punished and Becky was told to leave.

Since it was difficult for Miss Minchin to find a girl who would work so hard, Becky stayed. The girls knew that Miss Minchin also had reasons for keeping Sara, too.

"She's growing and learning so quickly," said Jessie to Lavinia. "It won't be long before she will be made a teacher. Why did you tell on her, Lavinia?"

"I felt I should," she said. "It's ridiculous that Sara should pretend to be so grand in her rags. And it's disgusting of her to share with servant girls. It's a wonder Miss Minchin didn't turn Sara out on the street, even if she does want her for a teacher."

"Where would she go then?" asked Jessie nervously.

"How do I know?" snapped Lavinia. "Well, she will look quite ashamed when she comes into the schoolroom this morning. She had no meals yesterday and won't have any today."

"Well, I think that's terrible," said Jessie. "They have no right to starve her."

When Sara came to the kitchen the next morning, she found Becky scrubbing a pot.

"The blanket was there when I woke up, miss,"

Becky whispered with a grin. "It was as real as it was last night."

"So was mine," said Sara. "I even ate some of the leftovers for breakfast."

Becky's eyes grew big. But when the cook walked by, she quickly went back to her work.

Just like Lavinia, Miss Minchin also expected Sara to look ashamed and hungry when she came into the schoolroom that day. Sara had never seemed to mind her punishments, which made Miss Minchin angry. But today Miss Minchin thought Sara would act differently. She expected her to have red eyes and an unhappy face.

When Sara entered the schoolroom she had color in her cheeks, a bounce in her walk, and a smile on her face. Miss Minchin was furious. She called Sara to her desk at once.

"Do you know that you are in serious trouble?"

"Why, yes, Miss Minchin," said Sara. "I know that I am."

"Don't forget it," said Miss Minchin. "And remember you get no food today."

"Yes, Miss Minchin," Sara answered.

"She can't be very hungry," whispered Lavinia. "Just look at her. She looks like she's pretending she's had a good breakfast."

Sara knew that the magic of last night must be

kept a secret. She was sent on errands in the most terrible cold weather that day. The cook was especially mean to her, but it didn't matter to Sara. The dinner of last night had given her strength. She knew she would sleep well in her warm, comfortable bed at the end of the day.

When Sara climbed the stairs that night it was very late. She stood before her attic door. Her heart was beating quickly.

It might all be taken away, she thought.

She took a deep breath, opened the door, and went in. Sara gasped. The magic had been there again! Even more new things had arrived—more cups and plates, this time for Becky, too; a scarf for the mantel; fabric to cover the walls; and big cushions for seats. A hot meal was on the table and a fire was blazing in the fireplace.

Sara moved slowly and looked around again. *Is this my attic?* she thought. *This is a fairy tale come true.*

Sara knocked on the wall for Becky. When she arrived, Becky almost fell to the floor. "Oh, my!" was all she could say.

That night Becky and Sara had dinner by the fire. When Sara went to bed, she found she had a new thick mattress and downy soft pillows. Her old mattress had been moved to Becky's room. Becky had never felt such luxury.

"Where does it all come from?" asked Becky.

"Let's not even *ask*," said Sara.

From that time on, life became better and better. Something new arrived each day. In a short time, the attic was a beautiful little room filled with lovely things. Each night a hot meal lay on the table.

The rest of Sara's life, however, had not changed. Miss Minchin was as mean as ever, and the servants were rude to her. Sara was not allowed to speak to Ermengarde and Lottie. Lavinia continued to make fun of Sara's shabby clothes. But it didn't matter. Sara was living in a wonderful fairy tale.

Day by day, Sara got stronger. She didn't look as thin, and the pink came back in her cheeks. She slept well every night.

Miss Minchin did not like what she saw. "Sara Crewe looks wonderful," said Miss Minchin to her sister one day.

"Yes," answered Miss Amelia carefully. "She is absolutely fattening. She was beginning to look like a little starved crow."

"There's no reason she should look starved!" cried Miss Minchin. "She always had plenty to eat."

"Of—of course," said Miss Amelia, seeing she had said the wrong thing as usual.

~ 19 ~
The Visitor

Then another wonderful thing happened. A man came to the door with boxes addressed, "To the Little Girl in the right-hand attic." As Sara opened the door to receive them, Miss Minchin saw her.

"Take those things to the young lady to whom they belong," she said to Sara nastily. "Don't just stand there staring."

"They belong to me," said Sara.

"To you?" said Miss Minchin. "What do you mean?"

"I don't know where they came from," said Sara, "but they are addressed to me." She showed Miss Minchin.

"Open them," ordered Miss Minchin.

So Sara did. She found comfortable, pretty clothing—shoes, stockings, gloves, and a warm beautiful coat. There was a hat and an umbrella, too. They were all expensive, well-made things. On the pocket of the coat was a note: "To be worn every day. More clothing will come when needed."

Miss Minchin was worried. Could she have made a mistake? Maybe Sara had a relative who found out where she was. It would be terrible if this relative learned the truth about how Sara had been treated. Miss Minchin looked sideways at Sara. She looked at her thin shabby clothes. She thought about Sara's hard work and the little bit of food she got.

"Well," said Miss Minchin quickly, "someone is very kind to you. You may put these clothes on now. When you are dressed, come to class. You do not need to do more errands today."

Miss Minchin's voice sounded as sweet as when Sara's father was alive. Sara was going to be a student in the classroom today! She was very excited. A few minutes later, Sara walked into the schoolroom wearing her new clothes.

The entire school stared.

"My word!" cried Jessie, elbowing Lavinia. "Look at Princess Sara!"

Everybody kept looking. Lavinia turned quite red. She did not look like the Sara they had seen only a few hours ago. She wore a dress even Lavinia was jealous of.

"Sara," Miss Minchin said, "come and sit here." She pointed to the seat next to her—the seat of honor.

The schoolgirls followed Sara with their eyes.

She sat down quietly and began studying her books.

That night Sara sat with Becky and thought about her mysterious friend. "I don't think he wants me to find out who he is. But I want to thank him—to tell him how happy he has made me."

Sara remembered seeing writing paper and envelopes that the friend had left. So she wrote a note:

> I know you want to keep yourself a secret. I hope you don't think I am rude by writing to you. I only want to thank you for being so kind. You've made everything a fairy tale. Becky and I used to be so lonely and cold and hungry. And now we are so happy and comfortable. Thank you—thank you—thank you!
>
> The Little Girl in the Attic

The next morning Sara left the note on the table. In the evening it had been taken away with the dishes. She felt better knowing her friend knew how happy she was.

Sara was reading to Becky that night when they heard a noise. It came from the skylight.

"Something's there, miss," said Becky quietly.

"Yes," said Sara. "It sounds like a cat scratching to get in."

Sara went to the window and opened the skylight carefully. Then she smiled. On the roof in the snow was the little monkey. He was crouching and shivering from the cold.

"It's too cold for a monkey to be out," said Sara gently to him. "You must have gotten away from the attic next door."

Sara slowly put her hand out to him. He had felt human love from Ram Dass's hands and he could feel it in Sara's hands, too. Sara brought the monkey inside. He snuggled up to her chest as she held him in her arms near the fire.

"What should we do with him, miss?" Becky asked.

"I will keep him with me tonight," said Sara, "and take him back to the Indian gentleman in the morning."

~ 20 ~
"It Is the Child!"

The next day three children from the Large Family, Janet, Nora, and Donald, sat in the Indian gentleman's library. They were trying to cheer him up.

The Indian gentleman was waiting anxiously for Mr. Carmichael. He was coming home from Moscow today. Janet stood next to Mr. Carrisford and patted his shoulder.

"It won't be long now," she said. "May we talk about the little lost girl?"

"I don't think I can talk of anything else," said Mr. Carrisford. "I can hardly wait to hear your father's news."

"Is it true that the little girl's father gave all of his money to a friend to put in diamond mines?" asked Nora. "And then the friend thought he lost it all and ran away because he felt like a robber?"

Mr. Carrisford took her hand in his. "But he wasn't a robber," he said quietly.

"I feel sorry for the friend," said Janet. "He didn't mean to do it and it must have broken his heart."

73

Then she glanced at the window. "There's the cab!" she cried. "It's Papa!"

They all ran to the window to look out.

"Yes, it's Papa," said Donald. "But there is no little girl."

The children ran into the hall to greet their father. Mr. Carrisford sank into his chair.

When Mr. Carmichael came into the room, he could see in Mr. Carrisford's eyes how eager he was to hear the news.

"The child the Russian people adopted was not the child we were looking for," said Mr. Carmichael steadily. "She was much younger than Captain Crewe's girl."

How tired and sad the Indian gentleman looked! "The search must begin again," he said. "Please sit down."

Mr. Carmichael sat and looked at his friend. He knew how much the Indian gentleman wanted to find the child and fix his mistake. "We will find her," he said.

"We must begin at once," said Mr. Carrisford. "Do you have any new ideas?"

"We have searched schools in Paris," said Mr. Carmichael. "Let us try London."

"Well, there are plenty of schools in London," said Mr. Carrisford. "There is even one next door."

"Then let's begin there," said Mr. Carmichael.

"There is a child there," said the Indian gentleman. "But she is not a student. She is a sad creature unlike Sara Crewe would be."

The magic must have been at work again. For at that moment, Ram Dass came into the room. He bowed respectfully.

"Sahib," he said. "The child herself has come—she brings the monkey who ran away to her attic again. Shall I bring her in?"

"Yes," said Mr. Carrisford. "Please do."

The Indian gentleman turned to Mr. Carmichael and told him of the girl in the attic and how he made her room a nicer place. He had needed something on which to focus while he awaited news of the lost girl.

Then Sara came into the room with the monkey in her arms.

"Your monkey ran away to my attic last night," she said in her pretty voice. "I took him in because it was so cold. Since it was late, I thought I should wait until morning to return him."

"That was very thoughtful of you," said Mr. Carrisford.

Sara looked at Ram Dass. "Shall I give him to your *lascar*?" she asked.

"How do you know he is a *lascar*?" asked the Indian gentleman.

"Oh, I know *lascars*," said Sara. "I was born in India."

Mr. Carrisford sat upright so suddenly that Sara was startled.

"You were born in India?" he said. "Please come here." He held out his hand.

Sara went to him and laid her hand on his. She looked at him with wonder. Something seemed to be the matter.

"You live next door?" he asked.

"Yes, at Miss Minchin's school," said Sara.

"But you are not a student?" he asked.

Sara looked down a moment and did not speak right away. "I was—I was first a student, but now—"

"What are you now?" he asked eagerly.

"I sleep in the attic next to the scullery maid," Sara answered. "I run errands and teach the little ones."

"Question her, Carmichael," Mr. Carrisford said quickly. "I cannot." He sank into his seat looking very tired again.

The father of the Large Family spoke in a nice, kind voice. "What do you mean 'at first'?" he asked.

"When I was first taken there by my papa," said Sara.

"Where is your papa?" asked Mr. Carmichael gently.

"He died," said Sara quietly. "He lost all of his money and there was no one to care for me or pay for Miss Minchin's school."

"Carmichael! Carmichael!" the Indian gentleman cried out.

"We must not frighten her," said Mr. Carmichael in a low voice to his friend. He looked back at Sara.

"How did your father lose his money?" asked Mr. Carrisford, who seemed almost out of breath.

"He had a friend he loved. It was his friend who took his money. He trusted his friend too much."

Mr. Carrisford looked sad. "The friend might not have meant to hurt him," he said. "He might have made a mistake."

Sara did not know the power of her words.

"The news of it killed him," she said.

"What was your father's name?" Mr. Carrisford said. "Tell me."

"His name was Ralph Crewe," she replied. "Captain Crewe. He died in India."

Mr. Carrisford gasped, "It is the child—the child!"

For a moment Sara thought the man might die. Ram Dass gave him medicine from a bottle. Sara stood near him, trembling.

"What child am I?" she asked slowly.

"Mr. Carrisford was your father's friend," said

Mr. Carmichael. "Do not be afraid. We have been looking for you for two years."

Sara put her hand up to her forehead. Her mouth quivered.

"I was at Miss Minchin's all along," she whispered. "Just on the other side of the wall."

~ 21 ~

All Is Explained

Mr. Carrisford had been so shocked at finding Sara that he needed to rest. Janet took Sara into the next room.

"I feel as if I don't want to lose sight of her," said Mr. Carmichael.

"I will take care of her," said Janet. "And Mama is coming from across the street."

Her brother Donald stared at Sara. "If I had just asked you what your name was when I gave you my coin, we would have known."

"We are so glad you are found," Janet told Sara.

When Mrs. Carmichael arrived, she hugged and kissed Sara. She explained everything as she held Sara in her arms and told her all that had happened. "You poor child," she cried and kissed Sara again. She felt Sara should be kissed often since she had not been kissed for such a long time.

Mrs. Carmichael explained that Mr. Carrisford had not really lost her papa's money. He had just thought he had lost it. And because he loved Captain Crewe so much, Mr. Carrisford's sadness made him sick. He himself almost died of brain fever. When he got better, he discovered that Sara's papa had died.

"And Mr. Carrisford did not know where to find me?" said Sara. "I was so close."

"He looked for a long time in Paris," said Mrs. Carmichael. "When he saw you pass by looking so poor and sad, he wanted to help you—because you were a little girl like the one he was looking for. He told Ram Dass to climb into your attic window and make you more comfortable."

Sara looked up at her, surprised. "Ram Dass brought all those things?" she cried. "Mr. Carrisford made my dream come true?"

"Yes, my dear—yes!" she said. "Mr. Carrisford is kind and good and he was as sorry for you as he was for lost Sara Crewe."

Then the door opened and Mr. Carmichael asked Sara to come speak with Mr. Carrisford.

Sara stood before his chair with her eyes sparkling. "You sent those things to me!" she said.

"Yes, poor, dear child, I did," he answered.

Sara knelt down by his knee and she saw a look of love in his eyes—a look she had only seen in her father's face.

"Then it is you who are my friend," she said with a smile. And she kissed his hand.

Mr. Carmichael turned to his wife. "Mr. Carrisford will be well again in three weeks," he said. "Just look at his face already."

~ 22 ~
"I Tried Not to Be"

In fact, the Indian gentleman did look changed. He was already planning things for Sara he had wanted to do for so long.

First, Sara would not return to Miss Minchin's at all.

"I am glad I do not need to go back," said Sara. "Miss Minchin will be very angry. She does not like me."

As if she had been called, Miss Minchin knocked on the door of Mr. Carrisford's house just then. She was coming to get Sara because a housemaid had seen her enter the house next door.

Ram Dass brought Miss Minchin into the room.

"I am sorry to disturb you," she said to Mr. Carrisford. "I am Miss Minchin from the girls' school next door. Sara is a charity student and has come here without me knowing it. I am sorry she has bothered you."

She turned to Sara. "Go home at once," she said. "You will be seriously punished."

Mr. Carrisford pulled Sara to him. "She is not going," he said.

"What?" exclaimed Miss Minchin. "Not going?"

"No, she is not going *home*," he replied, "If you can call your school a home. Her home is here with me."

"With you?" asked Miss Minchin. "What do you mean?"

"Mr. Carmichael," said the Indian gentleman to his friend. "Please explain."

The Indian gentleman held Sara's hand in his, just as her father used to do. Mr. Carmichael told Miss Minchin how Captain Crewe had been the Indian gentleman's close friend. He told her of Sara's large fortune from the diamond mines that had grown immensely.

Miss Minchin gasped. She felt that nothing so horrible had happened to her in her life.

"There are not many princesses who are richer than your charity student, Sara Crewe," said Mr. Carmichael with a smile. "Mr. Carrisford has been searching for her for almost two years. He has found her at last, and he will keep her."

Miss Minchin did not like what she was hearing at all. "He found her under my care. I have done everything for her. She would have starved in the streets without me," said Miss Minchin.

Then the Indian gentleman lost his temper. "She

may have starved more comfortably there than in your attic," he said.

Miss Minchin tried again. "Captain Crewe left her with me. She must stay until she finishes her schooling. It is the law."

"Miss Minchin, the law would not keep Sara with you," said Mr. Carmichael. "Only if Sara wanted to stay would we let her."

"Well then, I ask Sara her wishes," said Miss Minchin. She turned to Sara. "I have not spoiled you, but you know your papa was pleased with your schooling. And—I have always liked you."

Sara's green eyes stared at Miss Minchin.

"Have you, Miss Minchin?" she asked. "I did not know that."

Miss Minchin turned red and straightened her back. "Well, you should have known it. Miss Amelia and I always said you were the cleverest girl in the school. Won't you come home with me?"

Sara took a step toward Miss Minchin and did not take her eyes off of her. She was thinking of the cold, hungry hours she had spent alone in the attic. "You know why I will not come with you, Miss Minchin," said Sara steadily. "You know quite well."

Miss Minchin clenched her teeth. "You will never see Ermengarde and Lottie again," she said.

Mr. Carmichael stopped her. "Excuse me," he said quickly. "Sara will see anyone she wishes."

Miss Minchin knew that she could not stop the other children from seeing Sara if their parents allowed it. She looked at Mr. Carrisford. "She is not easy to take care of," she said sourly.

Then Miss Minchin turned to Sara.

"I suppose you feel you are a little princess again."

Sara looked down. She was a little embarrassed that her secret was given away in front of her new friends. "I—I tried not to be anything else," Sara said in a low voice. "Even when I was coldest and hungriest, I tried not to be anything else."

Ram Dass turned and led Miss Minchin quietly out of the room.

~ ~ ~

When Miss Minchin returned to the school she asked to see her sister. Miss Amelia heard the news with many tears. Timid Miss Amelia had always been afraid of saying something to make her sister angry, but today, she didn't seem to care.

"I always thought you were too hard on Sara Crewe," said Miss Amelia. "She should have been more comfortable and better dressed. I know she was worked too hard for her age, and I know she was only half fed—"

"How dare you say that!" cried Miss Minchin.

"I don't know how I dare," she said. "But since I've started, I'm going to finish. Sara was good and clever. She would have been good to you if you had shown her any kindness. But you did not. The fact was she was too clever for you. And you never liked her because of it."

"Amelia!" gasped Miss Minchin.

But Amelia kept going. "Sara saw we were nasty enough to beg for her money and mean enough to treat her terribly when it was gone. But she behaved like a little princess through it all."

Miss Amelia began to laugh and cry all at once.

"And now you've lost her!" She cried wildly now. "And some other school will get her money. And she could tell anyone how badly she was treated here, and we'd be ruined. And it serves us right. You are a hard, selfish woman, Maria Minchin!"

Miss Minchin was shocked. She could not think of a thing to say. But from that moment on, she realized that Miss Amelia was not as foolish as she looked.

That evening when the schoolgirls sat by the fire, Ermengarde entered the room with a letter in her hand. Her eyes shone with joy.

"What is the matter?" said several girls at once.

"I have a letter from Sara," said Ermengarde.

"There *were* diamond mines!"

Silence and disbelief surrounded her. "They were real," cried Ermengarde. "They were real!"

No one could control the girls' excitement and noise after that. Even Miss Minchin did not try. Until late into the night, Ermengarde read Sara's letter that told the story of her discovery. It was just as wonderful as the stories Sara used to tell to them.

Becky crept up the stairs a little later to see the magical attic room before it was taken away. She was glad for Sara, but she was sad to think it would be a cold, bare room again. She began to cry thinking that tonight there would be no fire, no lit lamp, no hot meal, and no Princess Sara.

Becky reached the door and pushed it slowly open. The lamp was glowing, the fire was blazing, and Ram Dass stood in the middle of the room smiling at her!

"Missee *Sahib* remembered," Ram Dass said. "She did not want you to go to sleep unhappy. You will be her attendant and can go to her tomorrow."

Then Ram Dass bowed to Becky and quietly slipped through the skylight.

~ 23 ~

Anne

There had never been such joy in the Large Family. Everyone wanted to know of Sara's adventures. Of course, what they liked best was the story of the pretend party and the dream that came true. They wanted to hear her tell that story again and again.

"That is my part," Sara would say when she finished. "Now won't you tell your part of it, Uncle Tom?" That is what Mr. Carrisford had asked Sara to call him. And he would tell his part of the story.

Then Sara would always say, "I'm so glad it was you who was my friend!"

And Sara and Mr. Carrisford indeed became the best of friends. Just as Mr. Carmichael had said, Mr. Carrisford was a different man in a few weeks. He was happier and healthier. He gave Sara little gifts tucked under her pillow and put flowers in her room.

One night they heard a scratch at the door. Sara went to open it. There stood a great big dog with a silver and gold collar that read:

I AM BORIS. I SERVE THE PRINCESS SARA.

Mr. Carrisford and Sara liked to sit by the fire together in the evening. One night he noticed that Sara sat staring into the fire for a long time.

"What are you thinking about, Sara?" he asked her.

"I was remembering a very hungry day and a child I saw. It was the day my dream came true."

Then she told Uncle Tom of the bakery and the fourpence she found and the child who was hungrier than she was. Mr. Carrisford was sad to hear about Sara's hungry days.

"I was wondering—" said Sara. "You know how you say I have so much money . . . Could I go see the bakery woman and tell her when hungry children come, to invite them in for something to eat? She could send me the bills. Could I do that?"

"We will go in the morning," Mr. Carrisford replied.

"Thank you," said Sara.

The next day, Sara left the house with Becky and Mr. Carrisford in the carriage. When Sara entered the shop, the baker woman looked carefully at her.

"I'm sure I remember you," she said to Sara.

"Yes," said Sara, "you once gave me six buns for a fourpence, and—"

"And you gave five of them to a beggar child," the woman broke in. "I've always remembered it. I hope you'll excuse me, but you look rosier—better than you did that day."

"I am better," said Sara. "And I am much happier, too. I have come to ask you a favor." Sara leaned closer and told the baker of her many hungry days and her wish to feed other hungry children.

"Why, it'll be a pleasure to do it," said the baker woman. "I can't do much, but I have given away many bits of bread thinking of you. You looked so cold and wet and hungry. And you gave away your hot buns as if you were a princess."

"The little girl looked so hungry," Sara said.

"She was starving," said the baker. "Many times since she's told me how much her stomach hurt on that day."

"You've seen her then?" asked Sara.

"Yes, she's in the back room. She's a big help to me around the shop. And she's a well-meaning, nice girl."

Then a girl came into the front room. Sara knew she was the beggar child. She was clean and neatly dressed, and she looked as if she had not been hungry for a long time. The wild look had gone from her eyes.

"You see," said the baker, "I told her to come when she was hungry and I gave her odd jobs. I got to like her. I've given her a home and she's thankful.

Her name is Anne."

The two girls looked at each other. Sara put her hand across the counter and held Anne's hand. "I am so glad," Sara said. "Perhaps you could give the bread to the children, since you know what it is to be hungry, too."

"Yes, miss," said Anne.

And somehow Sara felt she understood her, even though she said so little. Anne watched Sara as she left the shop with Mr. Carrisford. Then they got in their carriage and drove away.